The Woman Clothed With The Sun

The Woman Clothed With The Sun

Book copyright ©1999 by Fountain Publishing™
Illustrations copyright ©1999 by Anna K. Cole

All rights reserved. No part of this book may be reproduced or transmitted in any form or by any means, electronic or mechanical, including photocopying, recording, or by any information storage and retrieval system, without permission in writing from the publisher.

Published by Fountain Publishing™, P.O. Box 80011, Rochester, MI 48308-0011
Library of Congress Catalog Card Number: 99-72286
First printing 1999 in Colombia by Printer Colombiana S.A.

Book design by Lisa Alfelt and Daniel Eller of 7th Generation Studios, Inc.

ISBN 0-9659164-1-3

The Woman Clothed with the Sun

A story from the book of Revelation

Inspired and adapted by Bryn J. Brock
Illustrated by Anna K. Cole

With an introduction by Karin A. Childs

FOUNTAIN PUBLISHING

For my children, with love from Mama.   B.J.B.

To <u>all</u> my children, who have been nothing but
supportive about my work. A.K.C.

Introduction

The amazing stories in the book of Revelation - visions seen by the apostle John while exiled on the island of Patmos - have traditionally been understood as predictions of cataclysmic events that will one day take place on earth.

But not all have seen it that way. Emanuel Swedenborg was an eighteenth-century scientific genius who turned to theological writing in his later life. Swedenborg wrote that he was commanded by the Lord Jesus Christ to reveal secrets that had been concealed within the holy stories of the Bible - concealed until the time was right for the inner meanings to become clear. He wrote of these stories as symbolic, like parables, with timeless truth hidden within each dramatic scene.

Swedenborg described the beautiful woman in this vision as a symbol of a new understanding that would come from above, about God and the things of the Bible and heaven. This heavenly new understanding would be clothed with the warm and brilliant love of God, as the woman is clothed with the sun. It would rest firmly on a new understanding that was coming to earth, as the woman rests her feet on the moon. And it would be adorned with sparkling new knowledges, as the woman is adorned with a crown of stars.

This new understanding is pregnant, ready to give birth to new ideas about how to live life in service to the Lord God. But there is another character in the story.

A great red dragon comes upon the scene, a frightening symbol of forces and attitudes that wish to destroy this new understanding and its new ideas. These forces want to use knowledge - even spiritual and religious knowledge - to hurt and condemn others. The dragon in this story hates the woman and her child, and pursues them relentlessly.

But God provides protection in many forms, and the story of the "woman clothed with the sun" is a story of hope for the hearts and minds of all people.

A great sign was seen in heaven; a woman clothed with the sun, with the moon under her feet, and on her head a crown of twelve stars. And being with child, she cried out in labor and in pain to give birth.

And another sign was seen in heaven; behold, a great red dragon, with seven heads and ten horns, and seven diadems upon his heads.

His tail dragged a third of the stars from heaven and threw them to the earth; and the dragon stood before the woman who was ready to give birth, to devour her child as soon as it was born.

And she gave birth to a son, a male, who was to lead all nations with a rod of iron; and her child was caught up to God and to His throne.

Then the woman fled into the wilderness, where she has a place prepared by God, that she might be nourished there for one thousand two hundred and sixty days.

And war broke out in heaven; Michael and his angels fought against the dragon, and the dragon and his angels fought, but they did not prevail, and their place was no longer found in heaven.

So the great dragon was cast down, that serpent of old, called the Devil and Satan, who leads the whole world astray; he was cast to the earth, and his angels were cast down with him.

When the dragon saw that he was cast to the earth, he persecuted the woman who had given birth to the male child. But the woman was given two wings of a great eagle so she could fly into the wilderness, to her own place, where she is nourished for a time, and times, and half a time, away from the face of the serpent.

So the serpent cast water out of his mouth like a river after the woman, to cause her to be carried away by the torrent. But the earth helped the woman; and the earth opened its mouth and swallowed up the river that the dragon had cast out of his mouth.

And the dragon was enraged with the woman, and he went to wage war against the rest of her offspring, who keep the commandments of God, and have the testimony of Jesus Christ.

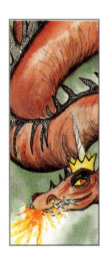

Then I saw an angel coming down from heaven, who had the key to the abyss and a great chain in his hand. He laid hold of the dragon, that serpent of old who is the Devil and Satan, and bound him for a thousand years.

And he cast him into the abyss and shut him up, and set a seal on him, so that he could not lead the nations astray any longer, until the thousand years were finished.

"Where she is nourished for a time, and times, and half a time away from the face of the serpent," signifies until the church grows and comes to its fullness.

From *Apocalypse Explained* by Emanuel Swedenborg

The text in this book was selected from the book of Revelation, chapter 12, verses 1-9 and 13-17; and also from chapter 20, verses 1-3. Special thanks to Rev. Andrew Heilman for advice on the translation. The final quotation is from *Apocalypse Explained* by Emanuel Swedenborg, paragraph 761. The deeper meanings in this story are discussed at length in *Apocalypse Explained*, as well as in *Apocalypse Revealed*, also by Emanuel Swedenborg.

The artwork was created using watercolor paints and ink on Waterford watercolor paper. The text was set in Tiepolo Book. Special thanks to Sarah Odhner for proofreading.